Lock the doors.

Latch the windows.

Then turn on every light in the house.

Can the electric company in your town handle the overload? Probably not. For added protection, arm yourself with an industrial flashlight. And lots of extra batteries.

WARNING: **Do not** read this book alone. Invite several friends over to spend the night.*

*Give priority status to friends with CPR training.

OTHER YEARLING BOOKS YOU WILL ENJOY:

TELEPHONE TAG, *Sherry Shahan*
A CREEPY COMPANY, *Joan Aiken*
A FIT OF SHIVERS, *Joan Aiken*
GIVE YOURSELF A FRIGHT, *Joan Aiken*
THE WOLVES OF WILLOUGHBY CHASE, *Joan Aiken*
IS UNDERGROUND, *Joan Aiken*
THE HEADLESS CUPID, *Zilpha Keatley Snyder*
THE FAMOUS STANLEY KIDNAPPING CASE, *Zilpha Keatley Snyder*
THE BOX AND THE BONE, *Zilpha Keatley Snyder*
GHOST INVASION, *Zilpha Keatley Snyder*

YEARLING BOOKS are designed especially to entertain and enlighten young people. Patricia Reilly Giff, consultant to this series, received her bachelor's degree from Marymount College and a master's degree in history from St. John's University. She holds a Professional Diploma in Reading and a Doctorate of Humane Letters from Hofstra University. She was a teacher and reading consultant for many years, and is the author of numerous books for young readers.

For a complete listing of all Yearling titles, write to
Dell Readers Service,
P.O. Box 1045,
South Holland, IL 60473.

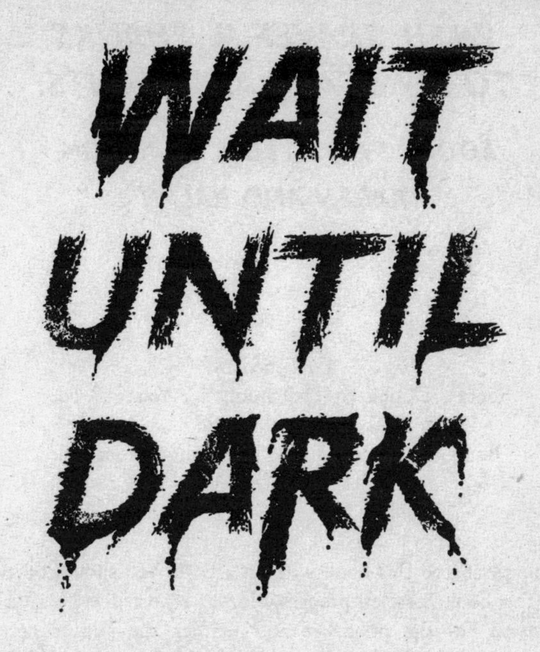

SEVEN SCARY SLEEPOVER STORIES

SHERRY SHAHAN

A YEARLING BOOK

WITH GRAVEFUL THANKS TO MY SCARY ASSISTANTS:

EDDIE, SYLVIA, LOU, BRANDON, KAREN AND RALPH

Published by
Bantam Doubleday Dell Books for Young Readers
a division of
Bantam Doubleday Dell Publishing Group, Inc.
1540 Broadway
New York, New York 10036

ISBN: 0-440-41293-5

Printed in the United States of America
October 1996
10 9 8 7 6 5 4 3 2 1
OPM

CONTENTS

1

MIDNIGHT SNACK

Hailey O'Malley shivered inside her short-sleeved T-shirt when a raw breeze smuggled itself in through the doorjamb. Weird. The first few days back at school in September were usually as hot as a blast furnace.

Mr. Inkhorn, the seventh-grade science teacher, was in the middle of explaining the rules for the school's annual science fair. "This year's topic will be invertebrates—animals lacking a backbone or spinal column." He paused to point to the pattern on his tie—dozens of S-shaped worms.

"Don't forget," he added, "that also includes crustaceans and mollusks."

Invertebrates. Hailey remembered the rest of the definition from a crossword puzzle in last year's biology workbook. The clue was *a classification that includes all animals except fishes, amphibians, reptiles, birds and mammals.*

Mr. Inkhorn passed around a sign-up sheet spilling over with possible science fair topics. Most of the girls circled things like sea stars and sea urchins. Pretty little creatures destined to be outlined with colorful marking pens, all their body cavities neatly labeled with a computer printout.

Sugar and spice.

The guys snagged slithering creatures: slimy sea cucumbers and banana slugs. No posterboard or colored pens for them. Their projects would ooze trails down the inside of old shoe boxes, with broken shells or redwood shavings tossed in for effect.

Snips and snails.

Acne Alex twisted to study the list when it landed on Hailey's desk. "I know what you're going to pick," he said through a cloud of pimple cream. "*Shrimp.*"

Hailey had been the shortest kid in class since preschool, so she'd already heard every shrimp joke in the book. All were about as dumb as a pencil without an eraser.

"Eat a bacteria burger," she said, and pressed her back flat against the wooden chair frame, adding another inch to her spine.

"No thanks," he shot back. "I've already eaten."

"Very funny."

Every year Mr. Inkhorn directed the science fair. It was a big deal at school, partly because the winner and finalists were given a pizza party in the biology lab. The smell of mozzarella and pepperoni singed over Bunsen burners billowed through hallways, letting everyone else know they were on the outside.

But mostly the science fair was a big deal because the winners were featured in the local newspaper, complete with pictures of their projects.

Hailey scanned the list, considering her choices. *Octopus* hadn't been circled. She knew the eight-armed suckers sometimes flushed red when stalking prey. Tomato hornworms hadn't been chosen either. Both were colorful creatures perfect for pastels or water colors.

Her pen didn't hesitate. It zoomed in, circling *spider.*

"That'll take about ten seconds to draw," said Alex. "Or are you gonna cut out pictures from a magazine?"

Hailey ignored him and concentrated on a project to make the entire student body at Jacob Creutz Feldt Middle School stand up and take notice.

First, she had to capture a dozen spiders.

Leaves rustled in the distance, making a sound like little kids whispering in a movie theater. Knotted clouds leveled the horizon, promising a storm. Soon it would be as dark as a starless night. Weird. Especially for mid-September.

A rusty old toolshed teetered in a clump of bone-dry weeds at the side of Hailey's house. Hailey sidestepped old tires and empty paint buckets littered around the shed as she edged her way to the sliding door.

Most of the time Hailey avoided the storage

shed because she imagined creepy things lying in wait in the corners. That was ridiculous, of course; both of her parents said so. Still, she hesitated before opening the door because of the idea—and this was so stupid, she didn't tell anyone—that eyeballs as shiny and white as vampires' teeth would pop out at her.

Stupid!

The inside of the building smelled different than usual, foul and spoiled with other odors she couldn't name. Dirt flew up in a thick haze, whipped by the breeze outside. Her flashlight attracted a halo of flying bugs.

She switched to the high beam when something moved behind the table saw. Too late. Whatever it was disappeared into shadows heaped with mouse droppings.

What if the matted webs clinging to the ceiling was one giant web? She twitched at the thought. What if a mutant spider the size of an alley cat had spun the silky fibers?

What if *it* was lurking behind the stack of old car batteries waiting for a human being to nibble?

Stupid, stupid, stupid.

Stop freaking yourself out. Or you will end up putting pastels to posterboard.

Just like always.

No, not this year.

In the end it was a fairly simple maneuver. A quick flick of her wrist and *bam!*—she slapped an empty mayonnaise jar over a quarter-sized arachnid. Just as quickly she turned the jar right side up and covered the wide mouth with crimped foil.

As if on cue, the shiny black body climbed up inside the clear glass. Later, after she had gathered the other eleven spiders, she would look them up in *The Encyclopedia of Animal Life*. The red marking on this one's belly should make it easy to identify.

Back in the house, however, she couldn't decide how to kill the first specimen for her project. A knife wouldn't work. Her plan required that all body parts remain intact. Besides, her mom would have a heifer if spider blood spilled on the kitchen counter.

Hailey ransacked the refrigerator for a snack while she considered her options. As a straight-A student, she was naturally inclined to turn to a book for an answer. So that's what she did.

After she licked peanut butter and jelly off her fingers, she scanned the synonyms listed under *murder* in her thesaurus. None of the normal methods seemed appropriate for a spider. *Choke. Stab. Poison.*

Then she saw it: *Asphyxiate.*

Hailey quickly opened the freezer and set the mayonnaise jar on the top shelf between a seven-bone roast and a stack of chicken pot pies—the spider's red belly magnified a hundred times by the glass jar.

The spider should be frozen stiff in a few minutes. Once frozen, it would be easy to pierce with a skinny needle threaded with fishing line.

The next step in assembling her science fair project: A Spider Mobile.

In the laundry room Hailey searched the sewing basket for just the right needle. "Hailey! We're home!" her mother sang out in tune with the banging door. "Give us a hand with the groceries!"

Us, meaning Hailey's older brother, Marcus, who would've finished basketball practice by now.

A freshman in high school, he towered over all the other players, even the seniors—a statistic he held over his sister's head like a steel ball.

Hailey slipped the packet of needles into her pocket and returned the sewing basket to its shelf. "Coming!" she called, heading for the kitchen. "Did you remember the . . ." She was about to say "sour cream and onion potato chips" when she spotted her mother leaning into the freezer, her hands shuffling the stack of pot pies.

"What's this doing in here?" Her mother held up the mayonnaise jar. Empty. No spider. The crimped foil glistened in the ice cube tray.

"What?" Hailey decided on the dumb act. Sometimes it worked. Sometimes it didn't.

"And what happened to the pot roast?" Her mother placed an empty Styrofoam tray on the counter. A few pieces of bone and gristle were tangled in the cellophane wrapper, all a bloody mess. "Marcus? Have you been feeding stray dogs again?"

Marcus answered from inside a jumbo box of cheese crackers. "Why do I get blamed for everything?"

Hailey lifted the jar to the light and squinted into its smooth glass mouth. Nothing. Just to make sure, she held it upside down. Still nothing.

"The roast didn't grow legs and walk away," her mother said, as if reading Hailey's mind. Then she hefted a twenty-pound turkey into the freezer and, using the tone she usually reserved for cross-examining witnesses, said, "I want an answer. *Now.*"

"I don't know where it is," Hailey said. It came out in a low whine, like a leak in a basketball. "Marcus probably nuked it in the microwave for a midnight snack."

"Marcus?"

"Don't look at me," he said, spraying cheesy crumbs.

"Time out," their mother said firmly. "You can both go to your rooms until someone remembers what happened to the roast."

"But Mom," Hailey said, "I have to work on my science fair project."

"Work on it in your room."

What could she say? *But there aren't any spiders in my room?*

Last year when Mr. Inkhorn had announced geology as the science fair topic, Hailey had joined a bunch of girls who turned a beach ball into a papier-mâché globe. Continents forest green. Oceans aquamarine blue. Too perfect. The guys had constructed earthquakes and volcanoes.

Hailey would just have to wait until everyone went to bed so that she could sneak off to the storage shed and collect all twelve spiders at once. The sixty-ounce apple juice jar in the recycling bin would be big enough to hold them.

Except for the constant *chomp, chomp, chomp* from Marcus, dinner was quiet. Both parents had disappeared behind covers of national news magazines. Hailey just picked at her pot pie, half expecting to stab a severed cephalothorax.

Her mind drifted to the year before, when her science class had visited tide pools on a field trip. A marine biologist had spent an hour explaining the concept of autotomy—the ability of some animals, like sea stars, to shed their limbs when attacked. A new limb quickly developed in its place, in something called regeneration.

Hailey cleared the table while Marcus stacked the dishwasher. She wondered, Do spiders regenerate? It wasn't such a stupid question. A sea star was sort of shaped like a big spider. Her thoughts fell into a logical line: If a spider could grow a new leg in place of the one cut off . . . then was it possible for an amputated spider limb to grow a new body?

What if . . . ? Questions were still screaming at her three hours later when she slipped between her stiff sheets. What if the spider had escaped from the bottle before it was completely frozen? What if the spider's legs had been frozen just enough to be broken off when her mother had put the groceries away? What if each severed leg had grown a whole spider?

And if it had, then where did the spiders go? How did they crawl out of the fridge? Where were they now?

Hailey's alarm sounded. Everybody would have been asleep for an hour. It was the best time to sneak off to the toolshed to trap the other spiders for her project without anyone's questioning her.

Wearing her sheepskin boots and I'M NO SLOUCH sweats, she trudged down the hall. The feeling of being pulled forward overtook her halfway down the stairs—as if a rope were looped around her waist and someone were reeling her in, drawing her downstairs toward the kitchen.

It must be hunger pains, she decided. Dinner had been only a nibble on the crust of her chicken pot pie.

Inside the kitchen, the freezer door dangled open on twisted hinges. The light shined on the remains of the twenty-pound turkey heaped on the floor. No mashed potatoes or gravy. No creamed peas with pearl onions. Just a scattering of freshly gnawed bones.

Hailey trembled, surrounded by an eerie stillness that clung to the walls. Every goose bump on her body told her she wasn't alone. Of that she was deadly certain.

Then something went *swish!* and a cloud of dust flew up from beneath the refrigerator. Whatever it was vanished into darkness.

"I knew it was you," her brother said from the hall. "First the roast. Now the turkey. Talk about a frame-up. What're you trying to do? Get me grounded into the next millennium?"

"But—" Hailey strained to find words that would make sense. "I think it's—" She started to say "the spider," when Marcus stepped in a squishy lump that looked like ground-up gizzard.

"Gross!" His toes wiggled in the greenish goo. "Throw me a dishtowel!"

But she couldn't move. She was paralyzed by her own thoughts. If the spider had devoured both the five-pound roast and twenty-pound turkey, it didn't take a mathematical wizard to figure out its total weight: twenty-five pounds.

Suddenly the freezer door swayed, casting an eerie light on the wall behind her brother. "M-M-M-Marcus," she mouthed at him.

Hovering in the shadows were two, three, no eight pairs of eyes the size and brightness of bare lightbulbs, their gaze as threatening as an electric wire dangling over water.

Sixty-four legs the thickness of broom handles but as flexible as licorice whips lurched and swayed as if fighting a wind storm. All were covered with stiff brushlike bristles.

"L-L-L-Look!" she choked out.

"Sure bet," Marcus said. "I'm supposed to turn around so you can take off for the stairs. What do you think? I just flunked my IQ test?"

Her eyes were frozen on the squirming legs matted with prickly black hair. S-Spiders . . . ," she managed, but only after the tangled wad tumbled out of sight.

Hailey scanned the scene for some sense of what was happening. "The spider escaped from the mayonnaise jar . . . ," she muttered through numb lips. "Its legs must have broken off. . . . Spiders really do regenerate. . . ."

Her voice died as she realized that the spiders had slithered off in the direction of her parents' room.

Hailey climbed the stairs with slow deliberation, pulled along by a trail of spider prints on the floral wallpaper—the bloody marks closely matching the lush roses. Her heart shifted into high gear, shooting blood to every organ including her ears, blasting away like a jackhammer.

Out of the corner of her eye, she saw something move. She turned as it jumped on the back of her head. "No!" she shrieked, slapping at the thing tangled in her hair. Its razor-sharp teeth sank into her scalp.

"Ow!" Another swipe sent a fist-sized spider flying across the hall. It splattered on the opposite wall like a water balloon.

Hailey tried to scream. She wanted to scream so loudly the whole neighborhood would wake up. But when she opened her mouth, cottonlike thread spilled out. The sticky stuff matted the walls and floor, spilling into her bedroom.

She batted at the stuff oozing through her lips, trying to break away. But it was all over her. Twisted inside her own web, she was reeled into her room. Huge spiders clung to her walls, spinning a shiny net over the canopy bed.

Not knowing what else to do, she started to chew through the web encasing her. Gross! Using her fingernails, she ripped at it until her nails were broken stumps. Her cuticles started to bleed. Finally she cut herself loose.

For a moment she just stood there staring wide-eyed at the giant spiders suspended over the bed.

What was she going to do?

1. Scream.
2. Dial 911.
3. Or . . .

Hailey liked the last idea best of all.

In a dusty corner of the storage shed a pile of heavy duty ropes awaited her. An especially sturdy rope would be needed to string up each cat-size spider for her science fair project: A Spider Mobile.

She swiveled on the heels of her sheepskin boots and headed for the old storage shed. . . .

2

TAILSPIN

Austin strained to look past a man with bacon-slab biceps and a stomach to match stuffed into the seat between him and the plane's window. If the dude had been wearing a red shirt, little kids would have climbed on his lap and asked for presents.

Over the enormous belly Austin saw clouds as puffy and white as a clump of his mom's cotton balls. A choking wind coughed rain against the window in intermittent splatters. The horizon bounced like a seesaw as the 747 attempted to keep its wings level, and failed.

Somewhere down the aisle he heard a little kid

whimper, "Mommy? Are angels shaking the airplane?"

Clink. Clink. Clink.

The metal jaws of three hundred seat belts clamped over slotted tails beneath static red lights: FASTEN SEAT BELT.

Austin noticed that his sign was slightly different from the rest. Instead of red letters, his were as clear as tap water. A few drops oozed from his sign. Condensation, he figured.

Seconds later the soothing voice of the copilot seeped from overhead speakers. "There isn't anything to be concerned about," he said. "It's just a small amount of turbulence. Please remain in your seats while the seat belt sign is on."

Austin hated airplanes. Not because he was afraid of crashing. A plane wouldn't dare dive-bomb with him in it—a fact as deeply etched in his brain as his multiplication tables. He hated flying because the seat belt sign always seemed to be on between Los Angeles and Chicago. Besides, there wasn't anything to do except listen to music and read.

He usually traveled on D Days, an abbreviation

of Austin's cowboy boots, almost falling inside the boot, and he'd simply used the pitchfork to flick it off.

Austin shook out the bag. "I was just wondering. Have you ever been on a flight where all three hundred passengers filled their barf bags?"

This was something he'd puzzled over ever since his first flight last year, not long after his parents' divorce. "Where would you put them all?" he asked.

Tonya looked as stunned as a bird flying into a windowpane. "Put them?"

"The barf bags. Is there a special storage bin? Or a chute, you know, like a laundry chute? A tube that connects the main cabin to some compartment below? Or are they just tossed out the emergency exit?"

The idea of hundreds of barf bags floating upside down like mini-parachutes, splatting on major cities across the nation, made him chuckle. Maybe this explained some of the recent UFO sightings in San Francisco.

Tonya was no longer squatting beside him. She had muttered something that sounded like "smarty-pants" and left to answer another call light.

What was wrong with the question? he wondered. It was perfectly logical. Then he realized she just didn't know the answer. She was too embarrassed to ask someone. Wasn't that just like a grown-up?

Curiosity killed the cat, his mom often told him.

SATISFACTION BROUGHT IT BACK, he always replied.

That's how he said it, because that's how he thought about it—in bold capital letters. Maybe even in glow-in-the-dark ink.

His dad liked to tell the story about his son's first word. It wasn't *Mommy* or *Daddy* as it was for most toddlers. Austin's first word came out as plain as white bread: *Why?* In kindergarten when other kids were practicing *O*s and *P*s Austin was perfecting the question mark.

Austin fidgeted in his seat. Now what? With the seat belt light on he couldn't even go to the bathroom. He usually saved the bathroom for last because it was his favorite place on the plane.

One of these days, maybe even on today's flight, he planned to test the smoke detector to see if it really worked. He hadn't quite figured out *how* he'd do this. Maybe snitch a book of matches somewhere. And he didn't know how he'd reach the alarm. Maybe stand on the toilet.

Austin pressed the call button again. This time MIKE squatted beside him in the aisle. Mike patted his head. *If one more person pats my head,* Austin steamed under his breath, *I'm going to bite him in the leg.*

"Austin, my man," Mike said behind a fake smile. "No need to worry about—"

"I'm *not* scared," Austin said, aware of the frown in his voice. He couldn't help wondering if this remark was standard operating procedure learned in Flight Attendant School. "I just had a question about the air slide."

"Okay, old buddy. Shoot."

"If the plane crashes—"

The radar of three hundred passengers picked up on the word *crash.* A squeal rolled from First Class to Economy. It sounded like a cat startled by a vacuum cleaner.

Mike's complexion drained to the color of instant milk. "Shhh!"

"*Who* pumps the air slide?" Austin demanded.

Mike whispered, "It's automatic," and, in a voice that was much too loud, added, "Look! It's time for the movie!"

In a microsecond he had plugged earphones into Austin's head, flipped the dial to Channel 1, and disappeared into dimming lights, just as the credits of *Mummies from Mars* rolled down a dozen screens.

Austin couldn't believe it. *Mummies from Mars* was his favorite movie of all time. A horror flick about a monster dripping with slime and green mold who stalked teenagers on Halloween. The last time he'd flown he'd been stuck with two hours of *Partridge Family* reruns.

Austin considered pressing the call button, putting in his request for a few bags of honey-roasted peanuts, but he knew from experience that attendants never answered the third call.

The slump-shouldered mummy suddenly swam out of darkness. A slit in the moldy bandages revealed two human eyeballs staring with the glazed determination of a starving animal. The mummy's lips stretched into a disfigured sneer. White suds bubbled from the corner of its mouth, soaking the bandages unraveling on its chin.

Mummies had never before fallen into the time slot reserved for dinner service. Austin had figured it out. A horror flick was supposed to take the passengers' minds off airplanes—more to the point, off crashing.

Austin also noted that *Mummies* had the opposite effect. During the movie the number of white knuckles digging into armrests quadrupled. A phenomenon that escaped the attendants who spent the entire one and a half hours in the galleys behind drawn curtains.

A cheer went up at *The End,* not because the movie was over. But the seat belt sign finally died. Instantly three hundred *clicks* signaled a race to the toilets. Austin zoomed down the aisle to a line twelve deep.

Bummer. Now what? Find some matches, he thought. Then, after everyone returned to their seats, he'd check out the smoke alarm. He couldn't *ask* for matches. Too suspicious. Especially on a nonsmoking flight.

Austin slipped into his seat next to Mr. Talking Armpit, who was slurping a reddish brown drink. It smelled like lighter fluid. Two red cherries bobbed on top of ice cubes, about the size of potato bug heads—*bloody* potato bugs. The guy popped one into his mouth. *Ick!* Austin expected to hear the sound of teeth crushing a skull, but no jaws moved. The guy had swallowed it whole.

The next cart rattling down the aisle was crammed full of steaming trays. Your choice of cardboard chicken or mushy meatloaf. Everyone knew meatloaf was meat that refused identification. Sort of like liverwurst. People who ate it probably ended up on the endangered species list.

"What would you like?" Tonya asked in a forced friendly tone.

Austin's eyes bulged and his cheeks puffed in and out. For a moment he looked as if he was going to blow his groceries. Then he let out a burp as loud as a truck backfiring. "Chicken."

Tonya thrust a tinfoil-covered tray on his table. "*Bon appétit,*" she said.

He figured that meant "eat a big one" in a foreign language.

As he lifted a corner of foil, steam swirled up and stabbed his face with a thousand pinpricks. Airplane food should carry a warning sticker: CAUTION: POTENTIAL MELTDOWN.

Steam? He puzzled a moment. Sure, why not?

Austin unzipped his daypack and stuffed the covered tray inside before he headed for the bathroom. No one was standing in line. They were all busy calming their fears with meals-in-a-minute.

He slipped unnoticed through a folding door marked VACANT. The best part of the bathroom was its smell, the sweet bubble-gum smell of blue toilet water. Wasn't it weird? There wasn't any water in the toilet until you flushed it. He made a mental note to ask an attendant about it.

Then a rushing swirl of blue appeared like magic, and away goes trouble down the drain. . . .

Austin climbed onto the toilet seat and held his

covered dinner up to the smoke detector. Not close enough. He planted one black boot on the sink, wet with soap scum. The other boot nudged its way onto the narrow metal shelf screwed into the wall.

Carefully balanced, he lifted a corner of foil off his chicken. A white stream of hot vapor rocketed up to the smoke alarm.

Bull's-eye!

The bathroom was suddenly filled with buzzers. Buzzers? No, it was more like horns—honking horns. The plane did a hard rock-and-roll number, and the RETURN TO YOUR SEAT sign flashed under his left boot. His rubber sole was barely balanced on the narrow shelf.

No doubt about it. This was the *muther* of all horns. The kind a semitrailer sounded to make his mom pull off the road so that it could pass.

His boot slipped and pushed the lever on the toilet. The sole left black marks as it skidded down the inside of the toilet bowl. Blue bubblegum water swirled around his boot and soaked his shoelaces.

The hole was like a wide mouth with the sucking power of an industrial vacuum. It suddenly flashed teeth—sharp jagged teeth, snapping at his boot.

Snap. Snap. Snap.

The teeth took a chunk out of the thick leather sole before chomping down on the whole boot. The powerful jaws snapped again. This time Austin was sucked all the way into the plane's bowels. Swallowed whole.

He blinked blue water from his eyes and waited for them to adjust. But they never did. It was too dark. He splashed around in the dark pit filled with bubble-gum water.

Austin opened his mouth to shout for one of the flight attendants, then shut it when he gagged on the sickeningly sweet water.

His head thudded on the ceiling when he tried to dog-paddle to one of the sides. What side? Somehow he knew there weren't any sides down here. No ladders. No diving boards. No shallow end with wide concrete steps.

Austin kept kicking, but his drenched clothes weighed a ton. He felt like a drowning rat in a sewer—the sewer of a jumbo jet. His water-soaked boots kept sinking down, then kicking up. Kicking and kicking. Splashing more, swimming less.

Then he was caught in an eddy: spinning in circles until he was so dizzy he cried for the barf bag.

Before he knew what was happening, the water sucked him all the way under. An undertow whipped him in circles. First frontward, then backward. His lungs were ready to burst under the strain of holding in air.

Austin was on the edge of passing out when there was a sudden roar. Almost a blast. The automatic air slide had popped out the bottom of the plane. Blue water gushed down the slide. Fat suitcases and duffel bags tumbled into the night air.

Austin flew down the waterfall on a box marked FRAGILE. He spilled into the atmosphere thirty thousand feet above bright city lights. His mangled black boots flew over his head as he kept spinning in slow motion. His arms were eggbeaters in fast forward; an attempt to fall flat, like a sky diver.

For an instant he saw the open belly of the 747

above him. Staring back at him from the gaping hole was the fat dude.

In a farewell toast, Mr. Talking Armpit lifted a glass of dark red liquid. *"Adiós muther!"*

Austin coughed his reply. Blue water spilled from his mouth.

Thousands of feet below, commuters clogged intersections in rush hour traffic. Inside apartments, TVs tuned in to the nightly news. Microwaves heated leftovers. Baths were drawn for sticky-fingered toddlers.

As the city lights zoomed up to welcome him, Austin sputtered, "I'm coming in a bit early, Dad. I hope you're there to meet me."

3

FAT CHANCE

Honey Sumpter remembered the day it all began. A weightless note written in scrawled chunky letters and taped to her baggy sweatshirt: FAT CHANCE. Less than a week later, words snipped from a fashion magazine taped to her desk: FEED MY LIPS.

Honey spent lunch using pinking shears to snip the notes into a thousand pieces. Each piece was tossed into a toilet someone forgot to flush. "Someday I'll get even," she muttered over the swirling water. "Someday . . ."

"Blubber is an inherited trait," Margo Langford

had announced two days later to a packed cafeteria. "Take a look at her parents. They were so fat when they were in school they sat next to *everyone*!"

Honey Sumpter had smoldered over a triple-decker hot dog sandwich slathered in mayonnaise. "Hot dogs are nothing but pig lips and fat," Margo stated, then stomped her milk carton—nonfat, of course—and hurled it at the trash can.

Everyone had laughed, and then started to chant, "Oink! Oink!"

Honey drained her own milk, double chocolate, so that she wouldn't choke. It ticked her off to admit that Margo Langford was 100 percent correct about her parents. Mr. and Mrs. Sumpter resembled a pair of grain-fed hogs. Swag-bellied. Pot-gutted. All the adjectives listed under *corpulent*, "the condition of being excessively fat."

After school when Margo and her friends strapped on in-line skates, spinning off to the yogurt shop, Honey made a beeline to the library. Row three. Second shelf. DIET AND NUTRITION.

Over the last several months she'd checked out scores of dieting books, even one on digestive enzymes. With each new regimen she'd swelled another ten pounds.

"Maybe," she mumbled, "there's a new book. One I haven't read."

"Can I help you find something?" Ms. Sepulcher, the librarian, had a knack for sneaking up on kids. Like everything else in the library, she was silent as a shadow. Even outside the book-lined walls, her voice was less than a whisper.

Honey realized how she must've looked: a slab of flesh squeezed into the DIET section, eyeballs bulging from scanning tables of contents. Pitiful.

Ms. Sepulcher ambled down a couple of aisles, abandoning DIET for PARAPSYCHOLOGY. "Energy is the source of all power," she said.

"Huh?" Honey wobbled along behind her, wondering if this was an old Chinese proverb. "What do you mean?"

Ms. Sepulcher's ice blue eyes danced as she plucked a weighty volume, *How to Turn Negative Energy into Positive Energy.* "Regular diets don't work," she said in her usual flat tone. "Because all your *energy* is focused on the problem—food."

Honey's mind backtracked to the Doughnut-a-

Day diet. She remembered how one twisted sinker had controlled her life. *When* she'd eat it. *Where* she'd eat it. *How* she'd eat it. Hours passed while she divided countless sticky morsels on a platter. Before she knew it all twelve doughnuts had vanished. Before that day she'd never been more than a three-doughnut kid.

Honey cradled the heavy book. "You mean an *energy* diet?" she asked, rereading the title. "I don't get it."

"Pay attention to chapter three." Ms. Sepulcher leaned in as if she was telling a secret. "It's called 'Revenge Is Sweet.' "

Was it Honey's imagination? Or did Ms. Sepulcher's eyes deepen—for just an instant—to the color of her lipstick, bloodred. It was a chilling contrast to her blanched complexion and ashen hair. Some kids said Ms. Sepulcher's hair had lost its color when she was struck by lightning. Others said the lightning had killed her, and that she was really a zombie.

Ms. Sepulcher swiveled on chunky black heels. "Chapter three," she said.

Outside on the playground a blast of arctic wind

stirred up dried leaves, their lifeless veins snapping against asphalt and chain-link fence. With book in hand Honey shivered through a wave of icy blasts, aware that lard-butts weren't supposed to be cold—all that blubbery insulation.

Taking a shortcut across the soccer field, hunkered inside her sweats for warmth, she wondered how it would feel to play soccer. Or any sport, for that matter.

Three handball courts stood in a row. Solid concrete blocks had been built high to ensure that no one slammed a ball over the top. Honey stomped over the peeling painted line, hugging herself against the chill. Dread creaked in her bones. Something was about to happen. Not something good. She imagined a violent downpour saturating the book, but there wasn't a cloud in the sky.

Then she stopped cold, frozen midstride. A headless mannequin in floppy sweats stood swaying in front of the second concrete wall. Black sweats, just like hers. Probably size 40, just like hers. An extralarge bib pinned to the chest read SPIT HAPPENS.

In an instant Margo Langford appeared and pranced around Honey. Margo didn't even bother to hold back her laughter. "You are what you eat!"

"Lips and fat!" added Valerie Van Dyke, a skinny girl whose blond hair grew a foot every year.

"Oink! Oink!" Angela Worthington tittered through a pearly-white grin.

I will not cry, Honey chanted to herself. I will not cry.

"So, do you know who it is?" taunted Margo.

Honey didn't answer, so Margo answered for her. "Why, it's the new Mary Wollstonecraft Middle School mascot"—she paused to twirl on her designer sneakers—"The Incredible Bulk!"

I hate them, Honey thought as she shoved past Margo and her attendants, clutching the book even tighter than before. I wish they all were dead!

As if in response, a sudden explosion of thunder cracked through the bright sky. The earshattering *boom!* echoed between the library and the handball courts. Margo and her friends shrieked when a bolt of lightning pointed its white finger at the dummy, slicing it in half. The sweats smoked and sizzled until nothing was left but a heap of blood-red cinders.

Margo stumbled backward. "You're going to pay for this!"

Honey knew she didn't have anything to do with the freak storm. But she decided to bluff. With the book close to her chest, she used a tone as controlled as the librarian's. "Just wait till next time."

After reading the first two chapters of Ms. Sepulcher's book, Honey realized she needed to dump her ideas about diets. Instead of trying to lose fifty pounds, she would turn those same fatty pounds into muscle.

Transform negative into positive. Just the way the book said.

Honey begged her mother to sign a consent form so that she could join a gym, then spent the weekend shopping for the perfect outfit: shimmery black spandex leotards, matching tights, leg warmers, and sweatband.

She strutted into the gym, anxious to join the

other flabby bodies. But the room was packed with fuchsia and lime green toothpicks, all posed in front of a mirror admiring their flat bellies.

What are *they* doing here? She slunk back into the shadows. I thought gyms were for fat people!

Back in her bedroom Honey threw the book against the wall. Positive energy! What does Ms. Sepulcher know, anyway? She's so skinny her flesh is transparent, like a film of plastic wrapped over chicken bones.

The book thudded to the floor. It fell open to chapter three. "Revenge Is Sweet." A string of words flew off the page: "No calories. No cholesterol. No fat. Swallow it whole."

She picked up the book. "Revenge. A game two can play," it said. "It's time to even the score."

The book itself was quite heavy. Five hundred plus pages in reinforced binding. She hefted it again. Why not?

Honey locked herself in the bathroom and cranked the hot water in the tub to full blast. Standing on the damp tile floor, she pumped the book as if it were a dumbbell. Even though she was wearing a sweatband, her eyes burned with salty droplets, but it didn't impair her vision.

"Revenge," she repeated with each inhale. "Even the score," she repeated with each exhale.

Honey felt tired and sore—and, all of a sudden, full. For the first time in her life she wasn't hungry.

In less than two weeks her sagging skin began to tighten. Little invisible tucks pulling it up. Now when she flexed there was the promise of shape . . . the promise of muscle.

Now only one question remained: *How* would she get even?

It took Honey six weeks to finish reading the book, always pumping it like iron late into the night. Now she straddled a bench near the handball court, munching a Power Bar, and wearing her new long-sleeved T-shirt: BLESS ME, FOR I HAVE THINNED.

A bunch of kids lined up at the wall. Two paired off to play: Margo Langford and Valerie Van Dyke.

Honey watched with interest as they took turns

punching the ball. Long-limbed Margo could hit it from anywhere on the court by taking one or two steps. Yet she wasn't strong enough to slam it home. Valerie spent the entire game flicking her blond waves, looking over her shoulder to see who was watching.

Why can't I play handball? Honey wondered, licking vitamin-enriched carob sprinkles off her fingers. I don't have to be fast—just strong.

As soon as she stumbled into line the game stopped. "What do you think you're doing?" snapped Margo.

Beneath her new T-shirt Honey flexed her muscles. "I wanna play."

Margo stared at her with a twisted smile: *Who are you kidding?* Her words were just as cruel. "No blubber-butts on my court."

"Why not let her try?" Angela broke in. Then she patted Honey on the shoulder as if she were her best friend. "It'd be good for a laugh!"

The game began in a thunder of "Kill it!"

Honey knew *it* referred to her, not the ball. There wasn't anything she wanted to do more than serve the ball with such power that it would shatter the concrete-block wall. With nothing else in mind, she lunged forward like a 747 in high-tops.

The bell rang.

She'd slammed it! Beaming, she watched the ball knick the top block. With equal force it re-bounded and power-dived at her opponent. Margo leaped sideways, missing the return.

That's when she said, "Bell rang. Doesn't count."

"The bell rang after I hit the ball!" Honey screamed.

"Oh yeah? Well, just ask the others."

Valerie and Angela snickered. "Nope, bell rang."

The playground emptied quickly as kids skipped off to seventh period. Honey was the only one left outside. She pressed her cheek to the con-crete wall, repeating the game in her mind a thou-sand times.

On the other side of town a church bell chimed three times. Fifteen minutes later the school bell signaled dismissal. Honey snatched the ball and started to bounce it against the wall. Easy. *Pat, pat, pat.* Like a salt shaker tapped over scrambled eggs.

Margo Langford strolled by in sequined sneakers. "Look at Fat Chance!" she taunted. "She has a new friend . . . a handball!"

It didn't happen as Honey had imagined.

Muscles swelled.

Veins pulsed.

Blood boiled.

Her fist hammered the handball. The ball smashed against the concrete wall, splitting the top block. A chunk crashed center court, like a boulder cut loose in a rockslide. When it struck the asphalt the ground rattled violently.

Everyone on the playground stopped. It was obvious something weird was going on. The ground within a twenty-foot radius of Honey began to buckle just from her stomping feet. That had never happened before.

While others stumbled around, attempting to maintain their balance, Honey connected with the ball, a bit harder this time. Valerie Van Dyke, who was closest to the handball court, was the first to discover what was happening. First her foot twisted into a crack; then she tumbled all the way in. Without even a chance to fluff out her long blond hair, she was sucked underground, spinning into endless darkness.

The others caught on when Angela Wentworth vanished into a different crack. Then the crying started. Everyone raced across the field, trying to escape. Too late. Honey was slamming the ball now, and in a flash the entire block wall came tumbling down.

Another hard stomp followed, and the asphalt wiggled like a plate of black gelatin. One by one the sobs were silenced as they were swallowed.

"New game. New rules," Honey told the only person left. "Time to even the score."

Margo Langford had wrapped herself around the tetherball pole, as if that would save her. "I wanna go home," she sobbed.

Honey was as calm as a nap waiting to happen. She strolled leisurely around the pole. Little lines split off from her high-tops.

Margo yelped as she made a dash for the bungalows. But the only structure still standing was the library. The only person left untouched was the librarian. Administration building, cafeteria, two dozen bungalows lay in ruins amid twisted desks and shattered glass.

Honey didn't bother chasing Margo. Instead she jumped up and landed with all the force of her 175 pounds. A violent *thud!* swallowed the sound of Margo's last scream—a *thud!* of earth on bones. The echoing shrieks were almost too much for Honey. Almost, but not quite.

Honey Sumpter sipped her morning protein shake over the newspaper headline EARTHQUAKE DESTROYS MARY WOLLSTONECRAFT MIDDLE SCHOOL. The quake was recorded as ten points on the Richter scale, the highest magnitude of earthshaking energy ever recorded.

Honey smiled, knowing Ms. Sepulcher would be pleased with her.

4

ICE SCREAM

Sierra sucked a glob of relish off her finger. Baseball and hot dogs seemed to go together: foot-long dogs heaped with pickle relish and dripping with ketchup. "You couldn't catch a cold if it sneezed in your glove!" she shouted at an outfielder on TV.

"Take him out!" Josh said, adding, "You're too old to cut the mustard!"

Almost as if in response, the twenty-four-inch color console crackled with static, and the watermelon red jerseys of the Tucson Tornadoes drained to a colorless gray. Even though the air outside was hot enough to melt steel, a thunderstorm was always possible in the desert. Especially as far south as Yuma, Arizona. Losing electric power was as common as flies on meadow muffins.

"No!" Sierra shouted at the sizzling screen.

Josh jumped up and smacked the TV as if that would keep the picture from fading.

For the first time in Arizona's history the Suns had batted themselves into the number one position in the league. Now, during the final game of the season, the game played to determine the winner of the pennant—the team who would *whack!* it out with the Los Angeles Dodgers in the World Series—the power was about to go kaput.

Again.

The TV sputtered as baseball fans all over the county held their breath. And there it went: *snap, crackle, pop.* The air conditioner died along with it.

Sierra pushed her hands deep in the pockets of her hip-huggers, sending the belt down another couple of inches. Her lacy white midriff blouse flaunted a splotch of ketchup that spread like blood.

"Now what?" she asked.

Josh slapped his Suns baseball cap sideways. The brim drooped like a flag at half-mast. "Don't you have a portable radio?"

"Dad snitched the batteries," she said in a doomed tone, "for the flashlight he keeps in his car. The same car my folks took to town."

"What about my car radio?" Josh asked.

"That's what I love about you!" She smiled brightly. "You're always thinking!"

Sierra realized she had said *love* for the first time since they had started going together. Josh must've noticed, too, because his freckles quickly disappeared under a rising flush.

"Wait a minute," she said, stopping before she reached the front door. "I'd better check on Summer."

"Is she taking a nap?"

Sierra nodded. "She should sleep for another hour."

The ancient farmhouse had had two bedrooms and no bathrooms when her family had moved in six months ago. Bathrooms had been added first, plus a spacious family room off the kitchen. A bedroom for her baby sister would be added next.

Until then Summer's crib was in their parents' room.

Sierra tiptoed across the braided rug, which covered a hardwood floor that creaked like old bones. The last thing she wanted to do was wake her sister. Of course, Summer was absolutely adorable. Especially since she had learned to ask for ice cream. She said it while licking the air—too cute. But she was also extremely demanding. Always wanting to be carried piggyback.

Summer lay curled up on her side, wearing only a cartoon-stamped diaper. A dozen stuffed animals lined the bumper, all with sticky-sweet fur—the leaky remains of milk and apple juice.

Sierra resisted the urge to bend over the rail and kiss Summer. After the game, she reminded herself. But for a brief moment she felt an urge to kiss her anyway.

As soon as she crept back down the hall, Sierra spotted Josh through the screen door. He was in his baby blue, refurbished '67 Mustang, fiddling with the radio. Easing the door shut, she bounded across the newly varnished veranda and descended half a dozen steps.

The door on the passenger's side of the car received her with open arms. She slipped in next to Josh at the same time the announcer shouted, "It's a double!"

A *whack!* by the Suns. Josh's excitement was obvious. The car bounced up and down as though all the shocks and springs were miniature pogo sticks. When the Tornadoes scored the tiebreaking run, he shouted, "One step closer to the pennant!"

In his excitement he pulled Sierra into a close embrace. For a second she thought he was going to use the *L* word. Then somewhere down the street a cat screamed, and the spell was broken.

Now the announcer's voice was scratchy and distant. Maybe the receiver at the radio station was on the fritz again. It often happened in the summer.

"Of all the rotten luck," Josh said, trying to tune in the station again.

Sierra was first to notice the thunderheads—puffy and purplish black, swollen with rain, and stacked against the far-off mountains. The clouds hung without movement in a formless color that was the shade of yesterday's bruise.

She watched as the clouds changed. Darkened even more. Not a total darkness, but a dreamlike dimness. It reminded her of something. What? Nothing. Probably nothing at all.

Sierra pulled away from the back of the vinyl seat. Her white blouse was transparent where it was stuck to her body with sweat. If the electricity didn't come on by ten o'clock tonight, she'd ask her dad to pull her mattress onto the porch so that she could sleep outside. Unless it rained. Then the thick humidity would be washed from the atmosphere.

It started to rain slowly at first:

pitter

patter

"The weather forecast didn't mention a storm," she said. "It was supposed to be as clear as a church bell."

"We might have to read about the game in tomorrow's paper."

Josh fiddled with the radio awhile longer. Finally he just flicked it off. No matter. Nothing but static anyhow.

With the radio off there was that unmistakable silence: the few seconds before a storm hits, when even the slightest breeze gives in to complete death.

A distant blaze of lightning cut through the clouds. The lightning was so bright that it seemed like high noon on a clear day instead of late afternoon with ominous overhead clouds. After each blaze of light, Sierra counted silently, one one-thousand, two one-thousand, three . . . And the grumble of thunder followed.

The cat screamed again.

A wink of sun bounced off the Mustang's hood. Suddenly lightning swept over the house, turning the painted bricks from bottle green to steel gray. Thunder rumbled heavily. The raindrops turned to ice, little frozen pellets the size of peas.

"Roll up the window," Josh said, cranking up the glass on his side.

Sierra followed suit. "Isn't this exciting?"

Josh nodded, but his eyes looked worried.

"Just think," she went on. "It's my first thunderstorm since we moved to the desert. And it's so warm outside. That seems weird. If we were in the East we'd be freezing to death."

The hailstones were coming down harder and faster, solid bullets of ice ricocheting off the hood. Within seconds the frozen peas had expanded into golf balls: thousands of frozen balls hitting the ground and bouncing as high as the car roof.

"I feel like I'm inside a giant popcorn popper," Sierra said.

A deep, throaty wind mixed with the barrage of hailstones, making such a racket that she had to scream to be heard. "Maybe we'd better check on my sister!"

Josh shouted back, but no sound came out. He looked like a character on TV when the volume is turned off.

Then she held up three fingers to signify three words: *Check on Summer!* Maybe he had never played charades. He shook his head with a deepening frown.

All her excitement disappeared as soon as Sierra

yanked on the door handle. A steadily rising wind sealed the door shut. She pushed back her tumble of russet hair. Her face looked as pale as melted ice. Sierra tried to shout "I'm worried about Summer!" but that was impossible. The only thing she could do was mouth her sister's name.

Josh nodded his understanding.

Even though the house was less than twenty feet away, it couldn't be seen through the artillery of hail. Any thoughts of trying to scramble to the porch were squelched when Bruno, the neighbor's German shepherd, was blown across the driveway. His front legs were outstretched as if he was trying to grip the ground.

It wasn't possible for Sierra to think about anything or anyone except her sister. All alone. Probably wide awake by now. Who could sleep through this racket?

Sierra wondered, Does this type of storm rip roofs off houses? Josh had been born in Yuma County, but she couldn't ask him about the storm. Even if she cupped her hands and shouted straight into his ear he wouldn't be able to hear her.

* * *

Sierra and Josh had no way of knowing, but at the Yuma Municipal Airport winds were being clocked at seventy miles an hour. Airport instruments measured several gusts that whipped above the hundred mark. The needle showed the wind speed picking up, like a freight train that has lost control down steep mountain tracks. It had already ripped all the bright orange wind socks off the runway.

Going, going, . . . gone!

Before the end of the seventh inning, even those with radios had abandoned the game, lending their strength to sandbagging operations along irrigation ditches. Fields of cotton, ripe for September picking, were completely stripped—nothing remained but inch-long stubs.

Later the local newspaper would call the winds record-setting at 104 miles per hour.

Sierra's eyes swam with tears when she pictured her sister in the roofless bedroom under the stormy sky. Hailstones filled the crib in an avalanche of ice while Summer cried out *"Sara! Sara!"*—the way she pronounced *Sierra.* Sierra shivered all over. She suddenly thought, Maybe what we heard earlier wasn't a cat.

Maybe it was Summer.

Was it her imagination, or had the car started to creep forward? At a snail's pace, but still forward.

Josh quickly yanked on the emergency brake, a movement so forceful he nearly pulled his shoulder out of its socket. The gearshift was already on P for Park.

Still, the car crept forward.

Sierra's face was extraordinarily pale. Was this the kind of fear that turned people's hair white? Or did that only happen in movies?

The sky was aflame with a whiteness so bright that she had to cover her eyes. Zigzags of lightning flashed, white whips cracking out rumbling thunder. In an instant the clouds drifted apart, then dissolved. Silence. Dead silence. Not so much as a single drop of rain. It was as if someone at the Department of Waterworks had flipped the Off switch.

"Is it over?" Sierra asked in a low voice.

Josh hugged her close. "It's over," he whispered in her ear.

"S-S-Summer," she said.

"Let's go," he replied.

Josh straight-armed the car door and climbed out. The car looked as if it had been attacked by a thousand crazed construction workers armed with ball peen hammers. Totaled.

Sierra pushed ahead, holding Josh's hand. No paint on the house either, she noticed. The bricks had been sandblasted to their original reddish brown color. Bits of lawn were scattered between the countless gopherlike holes made by battering hail.

She bent down to pick up a pacifier—Summer's—and shoved it into her pocket.

"Hurry," she said simply.

Josh nodded and followed her across the shadowy porch.

The floorboards in the hall had buckled during the storm. A bumpy path pulled them down a dark hall. No electricity. No lights. Power might not return for hours. Maybe even days.

They raced down, down the dark hall. Faster and faster. Both of them were panting to the point of passing out. It was as if they were in the last mile of a marathon with a finish line that kept moving away. Sweat poured off their bodies. Gallons of water could have been wrung from their clothes. Still, the bedroom remained just out of reach.

"What's happening?" Sierra asked.

Josh shook his head. "I don't know."

The panic was like a dishrag stuffed in her throat. She was afraid she might suffocate before reaching her parents' bedroom.

Sierra barely swallowed her panic and called, "Summer? Are you all right?"

At the sound of her sister's name the floorboards suddenly flattened out. Sierra reached the bedroom first. "I'm afraid," she sobbed, fumbling for the knob, fingers cupping cold metal. "Afraid of what we might find."

"It'll be okay," Josh said.

If it hadn't been for his steady voice Sierra might have collapsed on the floor and blubbered like a baby. Instead she composed herself and pushed the door open. Its ancient brass hinges let out a dull scream—a sound remarkably similar to that of a screeching cat.

Sierra shivered. "Oh, no."

Josh just shook his head, eyes widening.

A large plate glass window had been blown into the room. Jagged shards of glass spattered across the floor. The window frame stared at them like an unblinking eye.

Sierra stepped all the way into the room, glass crunching beneath her open-toed sandals. "Where is the . . . crib?" she asked faintly. "It should be against the wall . . . the wall with the missing window."

She continued to crunch her way to the twisted window frame. A blast of hot air shot through the opening. It slapped her with questions. What if the crib had been sucked out through the window? What if her sister had been sucked out with it? Maybe she'd be found miles away on top of a neighbor's hay barn.

Josh moved toward the open closet. "Over here," he said. Shiny white rails peeked out from behind hanging clothes.

Sierra uttered, "Summer," in a weak voice. Then she scrambled to the closet, shoving the clothes aside. Her sister lay curled up inside the crib beneath a single sheet of glass.

"Not moving." Sierra groped for words. "She's not moving."

From another part of the house a door slammed. Footsteps followed. Frantic footsteps, like . . .

"Sierra!" her mom called.

"Where are you?" her dad echoed.

With little thought of cutting herself, Sierra reached for the glass. She shrieked when she realized it wasn't glass—it was ice. A thick sheet of ice, and so slippery she couldn't grip it.

Underneath it all her little sister lay frozen. Curled up in a tight ball with her thumb stuck in her mouth. Was that a . . . slurping sound? Was Summer sucking her thumb under there? Or . . . was it the sound of ice melting?

"Summer!" Sierra cried. *"Summer!"*

The more she repeated her sister's name, the faster the ice seemed to melt. It was as if the word *Summer* were actually radiating heat.

"Summer!" Josh joined the chant. "Summer!"

The ice was melting so quickly now that water soaked the sheets and pooled under the crib. But Summer herself remained in a ball.

Sierra jumped when her mom touched her shoulder. "Where's Summer?"

A small voice inside the closet squeaked, "Ice scream."

Sierra reached into the crib and picked up her sister. "You mean ice cream, silly," she said.

Summer shook her head wildly. "No! Ice scream!"

And somewhere down the street a cat screamed.

5

BLACK BOX

Jimmy Hogan didn't always think he was a telephone answering machine. He didn't always imagine himself twisted inside a box that was so small that his nose smashed against the sleek, dark wall and breathing was accomplished only through fierce concentration, Jimmy pulling in shallow breaths until he almost passed out. A head cold could be fatal. The sensation of suffocation was constant.

There was a time when Jimmy Hogan was a normal seventh-grade kid who spent his afternoons in the family room, biting his fingernails in front of his favorite *Vampire the Undead* video.

Yeah, there was a time when Jimmy Hogan was a normal kid like . . . well, sort of like you.

Jimmy slumped in his seat while his history teacher babbled on about the number of casualties in the Civil War. Jimmy noted with interest that the lifelines on his palms were no longer indented and flesh colored. Each crease had turned black and was a bit raised, like the black cord that connected an answering machine to a telephone.

He switched his attention to the veins running up the insides of his forearms. They were almost as dark as the wire web on his hands.

Would an X-ray machine show a jumble of wires inside his stomach instead of intestines? he wondered.

"Jimmy?" Ms. Schmidt said. "Did you hear the question?"

Jimmy stared at his teacher, who wore so much powder that he expected her face to crack. "Shall I repeat the question?" she asked, knuckles pressed against hips.

"Jimmy Hogan lifted off at four A.M. this morning," he chanted in a long dull tone. "Leave a message and a phone number. He'll return your call via satellite. *Beep*."

The class shifted from muted chuckles to outright laughter.

Ms. Schmidt's jowls shook in a fit of exasperation. Of increasing frustration were Jimmy's excellent grades. One hundred percent on all the homework; 120 percent on every test. The extra 20 percent resulted from the extra-credit essay question, which he always aced. "I will not tolerate this type of behavior one more day. If you don't—"

His bloodshot eyes, a deepening red from not blinking, now flashed. *"Beep. Beep. Beep."*

Ms. Schmidt impatiently crossed the room. Her face resembled a boiled tomato ready to burst. "You may spend the rest of sixth period in the principal's office."

Jimmy brushed past her, shuffling casually out the door. "Your call cannot be completed as dialed," he spat over his shoulder. "Hang up and try again."

The principal's office commanded an ominous corner in the administration building. There was a rumble of sound nearby as kids shuffled between sixth and seventh periods. Any "Hey, Jimmy! What did you do this time?" was answered, "*Beep.*"

Dummies. All dummies. Not one of them had a mind of his own. Followers, all of them.

Jimmy paced in front of the door etched with PRINCIPAL. He felt a jolt in his spine as if a low volt of delta current were surging through his bones. He stared intensely at the dark cords in his arms, now running up under his shirtsleeves.

"Awesome," he muttered, just as the principal's door swung open. "Way cool."

"Hello, Jimmy," Mr. Kingfisher said. "Sounds like you're talking these days."

Jimmy refused to be outsmarted by a blubbery dude in a Smurf tie—a real throwback to the eighties. Jimmy's blood-rimmed eyes flashed in a steady rhythm like two blinking lights. "The number you've reached has been disconnected. There is no new number."

Seventh period wasted away while Mr. Kingfisher tried to make him talk. But Jimmy had erased both his outgoing and his incoming tape.

All that remained was a crackling sound produced by atmospheric disturbances; a sound meant to drive adults insane.

Shortly after the 3:15 bell Jimmy strolled down McCloud Lane, his high-tops splashing in the murky gutter. In front of him a shiny new drain stuck out of the concrete, sucking the water down an embankment in a bubbling stream that spilled into some river.

Each splash sent an electric charge up his body, eventually settling in his scalp and steaming his hair. Was it possible to be electrocuted in a gutter? he wondered, as he continued to stomp soggy leaves and trash.

His hip pocket pulsed with the envelope Kingfisher had told him to deliver to his parents. Two blocks later the envelope was folded into a makeshift boat and sent on its maiden voyage down the drain. The note itself was scribbled on lined yellow paper. *Ummm, good.* Yellow paper made gross spitwads, like the gunk hacked up with a cold.

Jimmy knew he was in big trouble as soon as he strolled into the kitchen. The expression on his mom's face confirmed what he'd suspected: Kingfisher had called.

"What am I going to do with you?" she asked with a shake of her head. "You can't spend the rest of your life acting like an answering machine."

Jimmy poured a tall glass of milk and gulped down the yellow spitwad. He wondered if it would grow in his stomach. "Why not?"

Only on special occasions did he press Rewind, Play or even Pause for his mom. He'd learned not to push her too far—after all, she had custody of the TV remote control.

"Do you know what will happen if you keep this up? You'll turn into—"

"*What?*" he interrupted. "An airwave?"

Mrs. Hogan squirmed at the kitchen table, adding three cubes of sugar to a steaming mug. Fueling up for some kind of lecture, he figured. "Did I ever tell you about Edgar?" she asked.

Jimmy bit into a peanut butter and sliced cucumber sandwich, resolved to play along for a while. "Who's he?"

"A teenager who lived across the street from us

before you were born," she said. "Edgar always wore a black sweatshirt and knitted cap, prowling in playgrounds, pretending to be a buzzard. He stalked unsuspecting kids and squawked, 'Better not fall down or I'll bite your head off.' "

"Yeah?" Jimmy acted bored, although he was sort of interested.

Mrs. Hogan's expression mirrored the time she had told Jimmy that his pet turtle had died. It had slipped down the bathroom drain while she was scrubbing scum off the turtle bowl. Jimmy liked to think the turtle was alive and well in the sewer. Sometimes he pushed lettuce leaves into the drain for it.

"So what happened?" Jimmy demanded. "Did he really eat some kid?"

"We'll never know," she said sadly.

"What do you mean?"

"One morning his mother went into his room to wake him for school, and . . ." She hesitated, staring into her dark mug. ". . . the window was open, the curtains knotted in the breeze. All that was left in the bed was a pile of feathers. Edgar was never seen again."

"Really?"

Mrs. Hogan slowly drained her mug. "There wasn't anything to put in his coffin," she went on. "Except stinky black feathers."

"Can we go there?" Jimmy asked skeptically.

"Where?"

"To his grave," he croaked. "I wanna see it."

The fine lines around his mom's eyes deepened. "He's in a pet cemetery."

"Oh, sure." Now he got it. This was lecture number 101. Next she'll say, Edgar pretended to be a buzzard, so he turned into one. If you keep acting like an answering machine, the same thing will happen to you.

Jimmy snickered and jumped up from the table, knocking over his chair. "Give me a break, Mom! That's just like the story about the kid who crossed his eyes and they stuck. You must think I'm really lame."

Something deep inside his central nervous system went *tilt!* and an endless tape of messages spilled out. "The number you have dialed is disconnected. *Beep.* There is no new number. *Beep.* Hang up and try again. *Beep.*"

The next three hours were spent in his room. Solitary confinement. No remote control for the TV. No headphones for the portable tape player. Not even a floppy disk for the computer. It was quiet. Too quiet. There wasn't anything to do except think.

It wasn't long before the clock's constant ticking started to bore into his skull. It penetrated flesh and bone like an invisible drill. *Tick-tock. Tick-tock.* The pressure was unbearable, but it wasn't the pain that bothered him most. If his head cracked open he feared his tapes would unravel.

"It's all Kingfisher's fault," he snorted. "I'll make him sorry for calling Mom. What right does he have to always be on my case?"

Another thought stabbed at him. His mom would have recorded the conversation with Kingfisher on the answering machine, so that she could play it for Dad when he returned from his business trip. Both sides of the little chitchat would be taped—Kingfisher's and Mom's.

An hour before sunrise, he slathered his door hinges with hair grease so that they wouldn't creak. His mom was a light sleeper, especially when his dad was away on business.

Jimmy tiptoed down the hall past his parents' room. The house was quiet in a creepy kind of way. Streetlights spit shadows through the sheer curtains, creating twisted black images that reminded him of the tangled cords behind the answering machine.

A whiff of something disgusting slapped him in the face. An overpowering smell that reminded him of his mom's compost pile—always puke green and soggy under the canvas tarp.

Even in his flannel pj's and thick wool socks he was chilled to the bone. Something weird was about to happen—he felt it in those same icy bones—and he was more anxious than ever to reach the answering machine.

Don't look back, he told himself. But he did look. On the wall was the shadow of something too horrible to be shown on one of his *Vampire the Undead* videos. He shivered again and ducked into the family room.

The answering machine was as dark as everything else in the room. No blinking lights. No messages since bedtime. The conversation with Kingfisher would have been saved under Memo. Listen first. Then erase. Quick and clean.

Jimmy fingered the shiny black box, quickly locating the Play knob. A nimble twist to the left sent a white stream of smoke shooting out of the speaker. It smelled like burning hair. Maybe a couple of wires had got crossed. Or did Kingfisher bust the machine just by talking to it? The notion was so sweet that Jimmy chewed it for a while before swallowing.

All too soon the smoke was a cloudlike mass, thicker than any cumulonimbus he'd ever seen. It surrounded him, whipping his body into a human tornado. Every orifice was clogged. Eyes. Nose. Mouth.

Wispy fingers wrapped around his neck before he understood what was happening. All he could do was scream, "Somebody pull the plug!" His cries faded as he disappeared into the speakers.

Without even a chance to go to the kitchen for a snack, he was stuffed sideways inside the little black box, his eyeballs turned into blinking lights: On. Off. On. Off. On. Off.

* * *

Mornings always filled McCloud Lane with chirping birds and streaming sunbeams. As always, Mrs. Hogan padded off to the kitchen ahead of her son to prepare his breakfast. This morning she planned oatmeal with raisins and low-fat milk, and two pieces of whole-wheat toast with his favorite orange marmalade.

When she noticed the red light blinking on the answering machine, she shuffled into the den and pressed Play. At first the voice that spilled out startled her. "Help!" It shrieked in pain. "Get me out of here! I'm stuffed inside the answering machine. Help!"

Mrs. Hogan shook her head with a slight smile. "Oh, Jimmy," she sighed, "will you ever stop pretending?" and went on to the kitchen.

6

DEAD OF NIGHT

Kids were thrown sideways in their seats as the yellow school bus leaned into a steep mountain turn. Off the side of the road a canyon dropped thousands of feet. Would snow-covered pines cushion the fall of a bus crammed with thirty kids and all their stuff?

"Sorry," the bus driver said. "That one sort of sneaked up on me."

"Where did you get your driver's license?" a kid in back shouted. "From a box of Cracker Jack?"

Kayla's stomach lurched with the bus. Don't puke, she told herself. Not in front of the whole class.

The tires squealed around another hairpin

bend. Granite boulders the size of the school cafeteria lined the uphill side of the road. Close. Too close. If the windows had been open the kids could've slapped the rocks.

A Smokey the Bear sign wobbled unsteadily—the base of the sign had been smashed in, probably by a car temporarily out of control. Smokey himself looked a little bit sad, as if he were a prisoner locked inside the cracked wood.

Kayla swallowed the bitter stuff in her throat. Nothing was worse than being carsick.

Whitney patted her on the shoulder. "We're almost there," she said above the loud chatter. From across the aisle Brittany added, "The last marker said Camp Eco-Song one mile."

Kayla wished she could return their smiles.

The air brakes whined and hissed as the bus swung into the camp's lot and parked. Everyone pushed down the aisle dragging his or her personal gear while chaperons tried to keep the noise level below the sonic barrier.

Kayla hurried down the steps onto solid ground. She sucked in clean air and let it wash down her throat. "It smells so green."

Whitney nodded. "Yeah. And clean."

The bus driver was already outside, tossing duffel bags onto the icy asphalt as if he couldn't wait to get rid of them. Some of the kids made snow angels. Others bombarded one another with snowballs.

A few minutes later everyone was rounded up and split into groups. Camp Eco-Song had six bare-bones cabins, each with room for six students and a chaperon.

The chaperons went over the rules for the millionth time. "Don't feed the wild animals, especially the bears. And don't forget about the buddy system. Never go anywhere alone. Got it?"

"Even when you go to the john," another chaperon added.

"Talk about embarrassing!" Brittany said.

Kayla and Whitney grabbed their gear and zigzagged down a gravel path to the door marked BLACK BEAR. All the cabins were named after animals in the state park: Mountain Lion, Mule Deer, Rattlesnake, Coyote.

Inside their cabin a wood-burning stove shared wall space with bookshelves full of books about the region's plant and animal life. A map on the wall showed a maze of trails rated from easy to strenuous.

Back in the city a wooden structure like this would be called a shack and would carry a warning sign—CAUTION: ENTER AT OWN RISK. Parents wouldn't let their kids go near it. Let alone sleep in it.

Kayla pushed her duffel under the bottom bunk against the far wall. Cold air sneaked in under the door and around the window casings. "Want to go outside and explore?" Kayla asked.

Whitney dangled upside down from the top bunk. "Okay, let's go."

Megan, the chaperon, was across the room fixing the zipper on Brittany's sleeping bag. "Don't be gone long, you two," she told them. "We're going on a hike in a little while."

Kayla opened the door. "We'll be back in a flash," she said, following Whitney outside.

Sprinkled among the cabins were various outbuildings: a dining hall, a bathroom (with showers), and a small interpretive center with stuffed animals—*real* animals.

Pressing through the wooden-slat door of the interpretive center, the two girls entered a narrow room. It smelled musty, and a lot like death. No wonder, with all those dead animals, stuffed to look lifelike.

A plaque under a ferocious black bear standing on its hind feet read DIED OF NATURAL CAUSES IN 2199.

"That's weird." Kayla stared wide-eyed at the sign. "It's only 1997."

Whitney nodded. "Someone must've put the two in front, instead of after the nine. I bet it's supposed to say 1992."

A small light focused on razor-sharp claws that could rip through metal garbage cans. The bear smiled a yellow, long-toothed smile. Stuffed? Yes. But nothing like a teddy bear.

For an instant it seemed as if the bear had winked at them.

It's *dead*, Kayla reminded herself.

"How would you like to meet this dude in the woods?" Whitney said.

Kayla didn't want to think about it. "I'll take my chances with big bad wolf."

"All the better to eat you, my dear." A khaki-clad ranger stepped from behind a large bulletin board. "Let me know if you have any questions," he said with a friendly smile.

Kayla tried to smile back. "Bears don't come into camp, right?"

"Wrong."

Both girls had question marks in their eyes.

"This is their territory," the ranger said. As he spoke, Kayla noticed his fingernails—long and pointed with a brownish yellow cast. "We're the visitors here."

"But they don't bother people, right?" Whitney asked. "Bears like honey and berries and stuff. Isn't that right?"

The ranger chuckled while he related a story about a camper who cooked bacon for breakfast. "He wiped his greasy hands on the back of his jeans," the ranger said, clacking his nails. "Later a bear ripped off the back pockets *while* he was wearing them. One bear even ripped off a car door, because it smelled a Hostess Twinkie inside."

Kayla turned her attention to the pockets of her ski jacket, pulling them inside out, flicking off crumbs.

"Let's go back to Black Bear," she said, looking at the bear's thick fur. It was a matted mess, in need of a stiff-bristled brush. Why hadn't they drawn the cabin called Mule Deer? Or Chipmunk? At least they sounded safe.

"Try to come back next month." The ranger's words oozed like sap through a knothole. "We'll have our new display by then."

"What is it?" Whitney asked.

"I can't tell you what it is." He paused to scratch the stuffed bear with his ugly nails. "But I can tell you this: It'll be the best exhibit in the whole park system."

Kayla pulled her friend outside. "I think the ranger is a tree short of a full forest."

Whitney giggled. "No kidding."

Hundreds of icicles sparkled from tree branches

and the roofs of nearby buildings. A cold breeze blew snow across a maze of paths that zigzagged around the buildings. Rock music spilled from cabins to blend with the hum of hair dryers in the girls' bathroom.

The sounds were the same as those at home, except . . .

"What was that?" Kayla stopped, her eyes flicking from side to side, searching for the noise. "It sounded like someone running his nails down a chalkboard."

Whitney quickly scanned the woods. "It's probably just some of the kids playing a trick on us. Any second Josh will jump out and shout 'Gotcha!' "

A dark cloud passed over the sun, making it seem like midnight instead of midafternoon. Now they understood the buddy system.

Scratching sounds swelled all around them.

"Maybe it's a bear," Kayla said almost in a whisper.

"Where are the rest of the kids, anyway? Why isn't anyone playing in the snow?"

Although she tried not to show it, Kayla was scared stiff. "I don't know."

They heard it again. Now it sounded like a huge animal scratching its fur.

The noise seemed to be coming from the other side of the cabin. Maybe even from *inside* the cabin.

Both girls jumped when the door of Black Bear swung open.

"We've been waiting for you." Megan's fists were pressed against her hips, but she looked concerned. "The rest of the kids went on ahead."

"Waiting for us?" Kayla repeated.

Brittany and Ariel crowded in. "The hike, remember?"

"Oh, right." Kayla settled against the open door. "Did you hear anything, ummm, strange? Just a minute ago?"

"You mean the pipes in the bathroom?" Megan asked.

Ariel laughed. "Some of the guys almost wet their pants. They thought we were being attacked by bears. Have you ever heard of anything so stupid?"

"Yeah." Kayla nodded. "Stupid."

The sounds were nothing but old pipes, she

thought. See? There is a logical explanation for everything.

The girls from Black Bear quickly caught up with the others on the trail. The guys were telling dumb jokes, just like always.

"What's that on the trail ahead?" Cody asked.

Drew said, "No, it goes like this: What's that on the trail? A head?"

They all laughed. Except Kayla and Whitney.

At six o'clock everyone piled into the Chuck Wagon for a cafeteria-style dinner. Cody asked gross questions like "What happened to the insides of the animals in the interpretive center?" Drew twirled spaghetti on his fork, answering, "We're eating their intestines." Then Cody squirted him with ketchup. "I *vant* to suck your blood."

Now even Kayla and Whitney laughed.

After dinner the rangers put on a skit around the fire pit. All except the dude from the interpretive center—he just stared into the audience and filed his yellow fingernails.

Kayla shot her friend a look. "Weird."

The skit was about safety in the woods. The

kids had heard it all ten thousand times on the bus trip up, and another thousand times from their parents before they'd left home.

It wasn't any fun being so cold. Even with ski hats and gloves, hiking boots and wool socks, thermals and heavy jackets, everyone was chilled to the bone. The program broke up early so that they could return to the cabins and huddle around the stoves.

Kayla needed to make a pit stop at the bathroom first. "I'll go with you," Whitney said. "The buddy system, remember?"

"Don't fall in," Megan called after them.

Kayla and Whitney huddled against the wind and tromped down the crusty, snow-covered path. Icy cold penetrated the concrete floor inside the bathroom and the thick soles of their hiking boots. Kayla's fingers felt frozen, making it hard to unzip her pants. No wonder the pipes screamed when someone flushed the toilet.

Scratch, scratch, scratch.

Kayla swallowed an ice cube of fear. "Did you hear that?"

Whitney scanned the high windows with her flashlight. "Yeah."

"It's probably a branch scraping the roof, huh?" Kayla said in a troubled voice.

An eerie silence filled the room before Whitney said, "That's how Megan would explain it."

Kayla took a deep breath and coughed. It burned deep in her chest, the way a mouthful of too-hot soup scalds you all the way down. "Let's get out of here!"

Outside, the wind was raw and bitter. It nipped at exposed skin, turning it red and plump, like a vine-ripened strawberry. Their eyelashes were white and encrusted with ice. Would the fine hairs snap off if they blinked too hard? Maybe.

"Did we make a wrong turn somewhere?" Kayla's words puffed on the white air. "I think we're off the path."

Whitney's teeth chattered. "What? I can't hear you."

Kayla coughed again and tried to control it, but it only worsened. "I think we're turned around!" she shouted.

Whitney nodded and waved her flashlight at the tangle of white trees. It was suddenly quieter. The wind had died down.

Kayla was light-headed from coughing, and from thoughts of being lost. It was dark, so dark. Not even a flicker of light from the buildings. "Where *are* the cabins?"

"Let's follow our tracks backward?" Whitney's voice rose, turning her words into a question.

For a moment Kayla just stood silent; then she shined her light on the ground. No footprints. The marks from their boots had filled with snow. Even from her raw throat, her cries filled the forest. *"Help!"*

With eyes closed and tears trickling down their cheeks, they both screamed, *"Help! Help! Help!"*

When Kayla opened her eyes she couldn't believe what she saw. All her brain cells were frozen, including those that controlled common sense. It wasn't just the shock of seeing a bear—the stuffed bear from the interpretive center—but the total disbelief. No! This can't be happening!

"No!" She screamed out loud this time. "You're dead!"

Somewhere in the back of her mind she remembered the plaque: DIED OF NATURAL CAUSES, 2199.

Maybe it wasn't dead . . . yet.

Maybe they were the ones who were dead . . . or as good as dead if they didn't get away. They could scream all night long. But if no one heard them, then the bear would eventually . . .

Eventually what?

Her mind pushed away the obvious answer, afraid to let the horror of it sink in. In the light of the dropped flashlight she recognized the brownish yellow claws. *"You?"* she screamed. *"No! It can't be!"*

Whitney scrambled backward. "Somebody help us!"

The bear swiped at their jackets, snagging clumps of polyester filling.

The last *"Help!"* was lost beneath an avalanche of laughter, the eerie laughter of the ranger who told the story about the bacon-cooking camper.

The search for the missing girls ended after ten days.

Shortly after the rescue parties had dispersed, a

new display of stuffed animals appeared in the interpretive center. Taking the place of the black bear who DIED OF NATURAL CAUSES, 2199 was an exhibit of two twelve-year-old female *Homo sapiens.*

The ranger clacked his long nails as he attached the metal plaque with the inscription LOST IN THE WOODS, 1997.

7

CRASH COURSE

Elisa must've been asleep because she woke up screaming at the top of her lungs—a shrill, piercing sound, like a siren at the scene of a deadly car crash on the interstate. In her dreams, the wreckage of a shiny black sedan lay twisted on the shoulder. Her daddy's car.

She screamed again and stuck the back of her hand in her mouth, then chomped down hard and forced herself to repeat, *"Stop it!"*

Too late. Another nighttime sound: the frantic steps of her mom rushing across the kitchen linoleum, her slippers flapping.

Now the twisted bumpers and fenders in her dream appeared as shadows on her closet door.

They looked like crooked black fingers beckoning toward the double bed. Come with me, they seemed to be saying.

Elisa screamed again.

Her mother pushed into the room and slapped the light switch. "Wake up," she said, sitting on the bed. "It's okay. It was just a dream."

"But . . . ," Elisa started, then pointed to the shadows, lessened only slightly by the light. "D-D-Daddy," she stuttered. "I dreamed he was in an accident."

Her mother glanced at the shadows. "It's the new coatrack," she said. "I put it in the hall last night. Remember?"

The new coatrack? *Right.* Mom had picked it up at a garage sale on her way home from the office.

"But the dream was so real. And Daddy . . ."

"We just talked to him a few hours ago. He was safe and sound in a motel along the interstate, so there's nothing to worry about."

Elisa was a bit relieved; still she asked, "Can we move the coatrack?"

Mom nodded. She moved the wooden rack,

then brought Elisa a glass of juice. "Good night," she said with a kiss. "Sleep tight."

"I'll try," Elisa whispered back.

Elisa never went to sleep unless her door was cracked open at least a foot. There was something comforting about the quiet hum of the refrigerator as it drifted into her room from the kitchen.

Too bad other sounds were louder at night. Like the dust balls under her bed. Some nights when her head hit the pillow the dust balls turned into bowling balls, crashing into the metal bed frame.

Maybe that was why people all over the world locked their doors at night and pulled blankets over their heads: to escape darkness and its eerie sounds.

Another ear-piercing sound sliced the chilly air—the cry of Dirk in his crib.

With Dad out of town all week, Mom had 100 percent of the kiddie duties, including returning a headless Barbie doll to Dirk's crib.

Dirk usually said "Uh-oh" first, then threw the old Barbie doll. *Uh-oh* was one of his favorite games.

Dirk was expected to wake up at night because he was just a toddler, unlike Elisa, who was twelve.

Elisa chewed on her comforter, trying to block the vision of the accident in her dream. Then a dozen bowling balls started crashing under her bed. Dust balls! Nothing but dust balls!

Listen to the hum of the refrigerator, she told herself. But tonight the balls were shattering windowpanes (or was it window*pains*?).

Get a grip!

There was something else weird about the small space under her bed. So weird that it scared her to think about it. When certain things were shoved under the bed—most recently her favorite pair of tennis shoes and a full box of pretzels—they vanished. *Poof!* Other stuff had vanished, too. Lots of stuff. Did the dust balls eat them? Elisa laughed at herself. Her imagination always clicked into overtime at night.

The sallow light leaking in through the shutters announced daybreak. Sitting up in bed with cheeks still flushed from screaming, Elisa opened the shutters. Since I'm awake I might as well finish my homework, she thought, and snatched her notebook.

Two hours later she was splashing milk on a bowl of cornflakes and popping a frozen waffle into the toaster for Dirk. "Dirk *eat,*" he said in a tiny voice. Headless Barbie sat up on the tray of his high chair.

Elisa held up the waffle box, pointing to the letters. "W," Dirk said plainly.

Elisa couldn't believe how smart he was. As soon as she pointed to an object and said its name, Dirk repeated it. All his capital letters had been memorized at eighteen months, and he said a dozen new words a day.

Rocking chair and *vacuum cleaner* were his favorite words. Probably because they had lots of syllables.

Her mother rushed in already dressed for work and stuck a cup of instant coffee in the microwave. "Thanks for getting Dirk ready for school."

"School!" Dirk's face shined around his sky blue eyes, the same bright color as their dad's eyes.

"Will Dad be home on Friday?" Elisa slurped a mouthful of soggy flakes. "For my birthday?"

Her mother blew on her coffee, causing ripples. "Sorry, honey. He'll still be on the road."

"Why doesn't he get an office job? Instead of driving around selling insurance?" Elisa heard the pout in her voice, but she didn't care. "I wish he'd be home tonight for dinner."

Her mother sighed into her coffee. "Me too." Then she changed the subject by picking up Barbie. "Where is her head, anyway?"

Elisa looked away. Barbie's head had vanished under her bed. Elisa would much rather talk about her birthday. She had wanted a puppy for a long time. All her other pets had been caged animals: birds and mice.

"Can I have a puppy this year? P-l-lease."

Her mom's eyebrows arched. "Oh, Elisa. No one's home most of the day. And a puppy is a big responsibility."

"But I *am* responsible. Look how I help with Dirk. It isn't even like a chore. I *like* taking care of him."

"You are wonderful with him. But then, there's your room. . . ."

"Teenagers aren't supposed to be neat," Elisa said. "It's a hormone thing."

Dirk swallowed his last bite of waffle. "Hormone. Hormone. Hormone."

Elisa laughed. But her mom asked, "When was the last time you cleaned under your bed?"

Elisa shrugged. What could she say? The dust balls kept it clean? Because they eat everything under there? Chomp, chomp, chomp.

The idea should've made her laugh again. Instead she heard her voice quivering. "Please, Mom—"

Just then Dirk pounded on his tray. "Body up," he said, which really meant he wanted to get down. Then he did something he'd never done before—he kissed Elisa's hand. Before, all his kisses had been for owwies.

"Bowling ball," he said plainly.

Elisa heard herself gasp. "What did you say?"

Dirk chanted, "Bowling ball! Bowling ball!" while he danced around the kitchen.

"Where did he learn that?" Elisa asked, stunned.

"I don't know." Her mother stacked the dishwasher absently. "Maybe school. Or TV."

No, not school. Not TV, Elisa thought dully. She knew where. . . .

Elisa's birthday present appeared in a basket on the front porch. She couldn't believe how cute he was—small and fluffy even though he was three years old.

Elisa's thank-yous were shrill enough to pop her birthday balloons.

"Marshmallow," she said, announcing the name of her new dog. In the winter when her dad was home the two of them sipped hot cocoa in front of the bay window in the kitchen. Their mugs were always topped with plump marshmallows.

Her aunts, uncles, and cousins sang "Happy Birthday" while her mom carried in a chocolate cake topped with thirteen candles.

"Happy! Happy! Happy!" Dirk repeated.

Elisa laughed and tousled his hair, still cuddling Marshmallow. Only one thing kept the day from being perfect: Dad wasn't coming home for another ten days.

Elisa sucked in a lungful of air and made a silent wish before blowing out the candles: Please send Daddy home soon! He has to meet Marshmallow!

Elisa didn't have nightmares anymore. No eerie shadows on the closet door. No bowling balls under the bed. Just Marshmallow snuggled up beside her, keeping her safe and as warm as a cup of steamy cocoa.

Several days later, when she came home from school, Elisa called out, "Marshmallow?"

Marshmallow always scampered into the living room when he heard the front door close. "Marshmallow?" she called again.

Elisa thought she heard a noise in the pantry. She hurried into the kitchen and opened the tall doors. Just the usual junk: boxes of cereal and crackers, and tons of canned foods.

"Marshmallow?" she said playfully. "Is this a game of hide-and-seek?"

Then the sounds seemed to be coming from the

TV. From behind the screen. How was that possible? Unless . . . unless he was stuck behind the set.

Elisa slid the TV away from the wall.

Nothing.

It wasn't funny anymore. "Marshmallow!" she cried. "Where are you?"

Call Mom. Maybe she took him to the vet. Yeah, that must be it. Some kind of shots. She just forgot to tell me.

Elisa noticed the light blinking on the message machine. She pushed the button. Muffled whimpers spilled into the room. Marshmallow! Then, close behind her: low, guttural sounds, like the growls of a vicious guard dog.

Elisa spun around.

What's happening?

The menacing growls were coming from down the hall—from her bedroom.

Elisa skidded into her room just as a fluffy little tail disappeared under her bed. "Marshmallow!" she cried, dropping to her knees. "No! Come back!"

His whimpers saturated the room. Elisa slapped her hands over her ears. "No!" But the sound was trapped inside her head.

Elisa reached under the bed.

Something slapped her arm.

Bedsprings? Dust balls? Bowling balls?

What she saw was worse than any nightmare: a dust ball as big as a human head, with brown, cracked skin. It looked like a week-old scab. Bony fingers just like the shadows on her closet door wrapped around her ankle. They dragged her kicking and screaming into the inky shadows.

Then a voice whispered, "Elisa, honey. Where are you? We're waiting for you." . . . It sounded like . . . Daddy?

The sound was followed by Marshmallow whimpering . . . and Dirk's faint voice: "I'll kiss your owwie."

Dirk! Elisa screamed silently. Her shoulder thudded against the bedframe, and she tumbled headfirst into darkness. Her eyes adjusted slowly, blinking as she took in her surroundings: an auto wrecking yard. Piles of rusty car frames were stacked to the sky. All the windshields had spiderweb cracks—from heads smashing into glass?

Tears streamed down her face. She winced at the pain shooting through her shoulder. Shooting? Not exactly. It felt as if someone were stabbing the tendon with a thousand knitting needles. Was it dislocated? Probably. At least she was alive. Or was she?

Elisa knew she had to get herself under control. Little by little, she slowed her breathing so that she wouldn't pass out. She ripped the hem of her T-shirt to make a sling.

"Where am I?" she muttered. "Is this one of my nightmares?"

She found herself straining to hear a familiar sound, like the hum of the refrigerator in the kitchen. But somehow she knew . . . this was much more than a bad dream.

In the distance she saw a battered sign: NO TRESPASSING—VIOLATORS WILL BE LOCKED IN A TRUNK. Pieces of trash stuck to bent antennas and rippled like tiny flags. A beam of sun bounced off bumpers, hubcaps and smashed soda bottles. Elisa spotted a doll's head, its blond hair so stiff that it looked fried. She almost picked it up, then stopped, seeing wormlike maggots wiggling inside the neck cavity.

"Marshmallow!" She cried when her dog dashed between two rows of cars. "Marshmallow!"

Elisa hurried after him. He ducked behind a flattened pickup, just as she spotted her brother. "Dirk!" He was clinging to his headless Barbie. He also vanished behind the twisted wreckage.

At first she was terror-stricken, frozen like a deer caught in the headlights of an oncoming truck. Deep down she wanted to find them. Grab them both and hug them senseless.

Another part of her whispered, "It isn't safe. *They* aren't safe. Sneak up on them . . . slowly."

Elisa crept around a van that looked like an accordion, past a windowless sports car. She stopped for a second to look down a line of flattened auto frames.

She shuddered, hearing glass crunching under heavy footsteps. Someone else was in the yard. A larger someone. But who? A caretaker? Or the owner of the voice that had called "Elisa, we're waiting for you"?

The voice that sounded like Daddy.

She dropped next to a foreign model minus its doors and crawled across the floorboard. The filthy floormat pricked the knees of her jeans as she made her way to the passenger's side. The rotting seats smelled worse than a dead mouse trapped behind a wall.

Elisa heard Dirk's small voice close by. What was he saying? She couldn't tell. Then Marshmallow barked. Silence for another few minutes. She swallowed hard. Spit burned the back of her throat. Her shoulder was on fire, too.

The silence was strange and spooky. She pushed herself through the space where a car door should have been. Inch by inch she climbed out on the other side of the car. At the end of the row she saw a shiny black sedan. The hood and fenders were smashed in. But it wasn't rusty like the others.

Elisa recognized it immediately: her father's car.

"Daddy?" His name dropped out like a bone being dropped by a dog.

She stumbled toward the car. Daddy! He was in the front seat behind the steering wheel. Marshmallow sat beside him. Dirk was in back, secure in his carseat, his tiny hands clutching Barbie.

Elisa peered through the rear window first. Dirk shifted restlessly and said, "Let's go bye-bye." She screamed when she saw his eyes. All traces of blue had vanished. His eyes were jaundice yellow—the same color as spoiled egg yolks. And that's how he smelled, like rotten eggs.

Dad turned his head slightly. She could see his profile. At least his eyes are open. So I know he isn't dead. Please let him be okay, she begged silently.

His words came slow and deliberate. "I heard you calling me, Elisa. I came as soon as I could." When he turned to face her she saw his eyes. They were the same sick yellow. "Guess I drove a little too fast."

"Then it wasn't a dream! You really did have a wreck!" she screamed before collapsing in the dirt.

* * *

The following morning Elisa slept through breakfast. She would have missed lunch and dinner if her mom hadn't come in to wake her up.

"Elisa?" Her mom gently touched her shoulder. "Do you know what time it is?"

Elisa's eyelids snapped open. "Good morning, Mother."

"Are you okay, honey?" Mom touched her cheek as if she had a fever. "I hope you're not coming down with something. And your eyes? They look . . . well, sort of odd."

Elisa's smile was carved into an otherwise blank expression. "I'm okay," she said, rising stiffly out of bed. "We're all okay. Marshmallow. Dirk. Even Daddy."

Then she dropped to the floor with a thud. "Come down here, Mother. There's something I want to show you. Here . . . under the bed. Come on, take a closer look."